KU-730-479

C00 803 932X

First published in 2018 by Child's Play (International) Ltd
Ashworth Road, Bridgemead, Swindon SN5 7YD, UK

Published in USA by Child's Play Inc
250 Minot Avenue, Auburn, Maine 04210

Distributed in Australia by Child's Play Australia Pty Ltd
Unit 10/20 Narabang Way, Belrose, Sydney, NSW 2085

ISBN 978-1-78628-084-8
CLP150118CPL04180848

Printed in Shenzhen, China

1 3 5 7 9 10 8 6 4 2

A catalogue record of this book
is available from the British Library

www.childs-play.com

Errol's GARDEN

GILLIAN HIBBS

I'm really good at growing things.

I’m so good at it
that we started
running out of
room at home!

What I really wanted
was a real garden.

I dreamed about my garden a lot.

Then one day,
I noticed something
I'd never seen before.

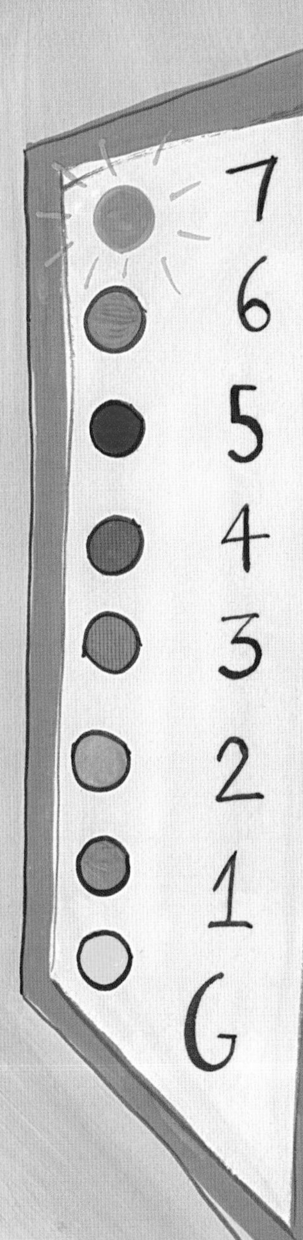

I always thought that
we lived on the top floor,
but there was another button...

...and there was a roof!

I couldn't believe
I hadn't seen it before!

This was the perfect
spot for the garden.

I told Dad and Tia right away.

We learned as much as we could about roof gardens.

But we needed help.

Luckily, everyone else was just as excited as me!

We made a plan.

SEEDS

Everyone had different things to bring...

which was good...

...because there were lots of different things to do.

And there still are!

I love picking all the fruit and vegetables.

I really love carrots!

Gardens are fun because they are always changing.

So, what will
we grow next year?

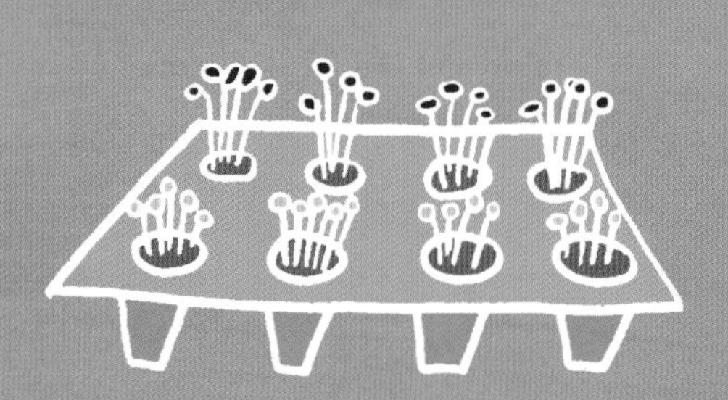